KidC .

America In Korean War:
A History Just for Kids

KidCaps is An Imprint of BookCaps™
www.bookcaps.com

© 2012. All Rights Reserved.

Table of Contents

About KidCaps

KidCaps is an imprint of BookCaps™ that is just for kids! Each month BookCaps will be releasing several books in this exciting imprint. Visit are website or like us on Facebook to see more!

One American soldier comforts another whose best friend was just killed in the fighting.[1]

---

[1] Image source: http://authorgarywilliams.net/?p=662

Introduction

Platoon Sergeant Daniel Adams ducked his head down to avoid the bullets that seemed to be coming from everywhere. To his right, a massive explosion rocked the earth and sent dirt flying in all directions. Daniel was pretty sure that he heard some screaming in English, but he couldn't be sure. Through the smoke and dust, it was hard to see much of anything, and it was harder still to know who exactly he was fighting against or where they were shooting from. He heard some more gunshots from up ahead and to the left, and ducked his head back behind the rocks that protected him.

One week ago, Daniel had been stationed in Japan, helping the country recuperate from the damage of World War Two. Then he had heard on the news that the North Korean military had sent soldiers down across the border to South Korea and that there was a lot of fighting. Daniel knew that he and his infantry unit had been sent here, to Osan, south of the capital of Seoul, to stop the advancing North Korean army. But he and his fellow soldiers weren't prepared at all to fight against tanks and artillery, both of which the North Korean army had. The Americans only had guns, no tanks and no heavy weapons.

Another round was fired from a tank; Daniel could tell by the louder boom, and he curled into a ball. The earth around him exploded, and he knew that the shell had landed just a few feet from his current position. He popped up from behind the rock and fired towards where the shell came from. The men on either side of him did the same. In the hot weather, they never stopped sweating, not even at night. They had no supplies, and they were drinking the dirty water used to irrigate rice fields. Daniels stomach had cramped up yesterday as a result, but the North Koreans sure weren't about to wait for him to feel better before attacking.

Daniel's men looked at each other through the smoke and the dust. In his Infantry Regiment, there were about 500 soldiers. The wind picked up for a moment and Daniel could see over to where the enemy was, and the sight took his breath away. There were more than 500 soldiers, many more. He saw row after row of tanks, and men lined up as far back as his eye could see. His immediate superior, his platoon leader, Lieutenant Dodgson, yelled out: "There's gotta be at least 5,000 of them, and a few dozen tanks! We won't be able to hold them off forever! What do they expect us to do out here?"

Daniel looked over at his Platoon Leader and couldn't believe it- he heard fear in the man's voice! Looking into the Lieutenant's eyes, Daniel yelled back: "Sir, we have to hold. Those were our orders. We have to fight to the last man."

The Lieutenant kept staring at the tanks. He yelled over the sound of the fighting. "We can't stop those tanks, Sergeant Adams. We don't have the firepower.

My radio's down, and I can't get through to the Captain." He looked behind him, then to the right and to the left. "No, we have to fall back. The rest of the regiment must have already retreated; that's the only explanation for the radio silence. It's been three hours, the odds are getting worse, and we've got no air support out here. We're alone, and we don't stand a chance. Give the order to fall back, Sergeant Adams. Give it now."

Daniel took a breath and then shouted out: "Fall back, fall back, right now. Leave your heavy equipment. Take only what you can carry and get going. Fall back now!"

The men of Company B looked almost grateful to finally be moving away from the advancing North Korean troops. They moved back towards a clump of trees where the wounded were being treated. As he bent down in order to pick up a litter that held a wounded soldier, the Lieutenant Dodgson told him, "No time, Adams. There's no time. Leave him with the medic. The North Koreans know the rules of the U.N. charter: that all prisoners of war must be treated with dignity. And they know that noncombatant personnel, like the medic here, cannot be hurt either. Leave them, there's no time."

Daniel froze, unsure what to do, and looked into the eyes of the medic. The medic seemed sad, but shook his head. "Go, Adams. We'll be fine."

Daniels grabbed his gun and ran, with the rest of his men, south, away from the North Korean soldiers.

He never saw the medic or the wounded soldier again.

Can you imagine what it would have been like to have been fighting in that battle? Called the Battle of Osan, it was fought on July 6, 1950, and marked the first armed intervention of American soldiers in the Korean War. The story we saw above actually happened, although the characters weren't real. Company B, part of the 1st Battalion, 21st Infantry of the United States Army, certainly was left behind when the rest of the troops retreated, and they had to leave behind their equipment and their wounded in order to get away safely. It was a scary battle.

Have you ever heard of the Battle of Osan, or even of the Korean War that it was a part of? This war has been called America's "Forgotten War" because not a lot of people talk about it. It was not global, like World War Two had been, and it was not as controversial as the Vietnam War. Although it lasted for about three years, and although some 40,000 American soldiers lost their lives, the whole thing seemed so far away that, to this day, not a lot of people even know what the war was about or how it ended. Sometimes, they don't even know that it happened. In this handbook, we hope that you will learn the most pertinent stuff about the Korean War. What can you expect to see?

First, we will learn more about what actually caused the Korean War. Did you know that the war actually started as a sort of civil war between the Korean people but that later other nations got involved? Also, do you know what the Korean War has to do with the Cold War that was fought between the United States and the U.S.S.R.? You will learn the answers in this section.

The next section will talk more about why the United States and other nations got involved in the civil war of a nation on the other side of the world. One of the biggest reasons was something called the "domino theory", something that genuinely scared the President of the United States. We will also learn what the U.S.S.R. and China thought about the United States getting involved in the war, and what they did about it.

After that, we will learn more about the Korean War itself. As you can see in the picture at the beginning of this handbook, there were some truly sad moments during the war, like when soldiers lost their best friends on the battlefields. The Korean War also saw a lot of soldiers and civilians get killed, and you may be surprised to find out who was responsible for many of the deaths.

The following section will tell us what it was like to be a kid living during the Korean War. We will use our imaginations to see what it was like to be a kid in the United States during the war, and what kinds of things they would have seen and heard about. Then we will see what it would have been like to be a kid living in Korea during the war. As you can probably imagine, it would have been a lot scarier in Korea!

After that, we will see how the Korean War finally ended. Although the fighting was pretty fierce and tough in the beginning, and although the armies moved around a lot, by the end of the war, things had settled down and everyone wanted the fighting to end. Even so, it took almost two years for the governments on each side to finally sign the documents that ended the fighting. We will see what conditions were finally met to stop the bullets from flying and the bombs from being dropped.

The section after that will let us know what it was like after the war ended, and will include some of the final facts and figures.

Before we read any further, you may wonder why you should care about a war that happened over 60 years ago. Well, in many ways, the causes of that war are still around, and a lot of people are worried that another war in Korea could break out anytime. As you probably know, the only way to avoid repeating the mistakes of the past is to learn from them. So try to learn what the factors were which led to so many people dying in the Korean War. That way, maybe we can keep the same thing from happening again in the future.

The Korean War was fought from June 25, 1950 to July 27, 1953. Let's learn more about this sad but significant war.

Chapter 1: What Led Up to the Korean War?

A young Korean girl with her baby brother walks by a tank during the Korean War.[2]

Why did the Korean peninsula erupt in civil war in 1953? Basically, the country was split into two halves after World War Two, and there was a fight as to which way the reestablished government should be run. But how did the country get to be split into two halves in the first place? Let's find out.

In 1910, the nearby island empire of Japan decided to invade and conquer the land of Korea. Until World War Two, the Korean people were totally ruled by the

[2] Image source: http://www.archives.gov/research/military/korean-war/

Empire of Japan, and they had no voice at all in the way that their government was run or in the way that they were treated. Once World War Two broke out, the Japanese used the Koreans to make their country stronger, and many Koreans were forced to go to Japanese cities and to work on behalf of the war effort. When the two atomic bombs were dropped on the cities of Hiroshima and Nagasaki in 1945, about 25% of all the people who died were Koreans that had been forced to support the Japanese war machine.

During the war, the Soviet Union (U.S.S.R.) had agreed to step in and to help the Allied forces stop Japan from taking over Asia. The Soviets moved in from the north, closer and closer to Japan, and made it all the way to the 38th Parallel (a circle of latitude marking a location) of the Korean peninsula, deep into Japanese territory. Once there, they waited for further instructions and to see how the Allied invasion of Japan went.

Once the war was over, it was decided by representatives in Washington D.C. that Korea would need some help getting on its feet and establishing itself as an independent nation again. After all, the country had been dominated by a foreign country for over 30 years. It was decided that the Soviets would care for the northern part of Korean down to the 38th Parallel, and the Allied forces (principally the United States) would take care of everything from there south.

World War Two ended towards the final part of 1945, and the occupation by the Soviets and the Allies followed almost immediately afterwards. The citizens of Korea had the same problems to handle as those of any country, but because of the foreign influences, the northern part and the southern part decided to handle their problems very differently. Although both sides wanted to be united together again as one nation, the northern part favored a Communist government (like the U.S.S.R.) while the southern side favored a Democratic form of government (like the U.S.A.).

Before we continue, let's talk a moment about the different between a "Communist" and a "Democratic" government. In a democratic government, like in the United States, the people have a lot more say in what and how things are done. They can decide which laws they want, who should be in charge, and they can elect representatives who will decide whether or not to go to war and with whom. Citizens can choose where to work, large companies can compete with each other, and individuals can buy and own houses and properties. A Democratic government responds to the people, and so it always tries to be fair and to do the right thing.

A Communist government is also for the people, but it is set up a little differently. Instead of establishing private companies and private property, the idea is that everything belongs to the community. Everyone shares the good that the community produces, and they receive from the community (represented by a small government) a house, a job, and enough food for their family. However, Communism looks good on paper (because everyone gets what they need), but it becomes extremely easy for a few bad guys to take advantage of it. Also, because there can be lots of problems organizing everything, this type of government tends to cause a lot of suffering and poverty in the countries that accept it.

You can understand that both halves of Korea, the Communist Northern part and the Democratic Southern part, both thought that their form of government was the best. However, some people living in the North wanted things to be more like the South, and vice versa. The governments of both sides were particularly mean to the citizens who didn't agree with them, and many were executed if they tried to protest or change the way things were done.

The border between the two sides, the 38th Parallel, became the focal point of fighting and tensions between the two sides, because it was where one way of doing things ended and another began. In the years after World War Two ended, there were lots of little fights (called skirmishes) between Northern and Southern soldiers, and lots of people died. It is estimated that about 10,000 soldiers had died by the time the Korean War "officially" started.

The world was taking notice of the fighting going on between the two parts of Korea, but there were two nations in particular that were truly interested: the United States of America (U.S.A.) and the Union of Soviet Socialist Republics (U.S.S.R.). After World

War Two ended, both sides looked at each other with a lot of suspicion. Because the United States thought that everybody should have a democratic government and because the Soviets thought that everybody should have a communist government, the two sides both thought that the other was about to start a war. They started building up their piles of weapons and getting ready for a fight. This came to be known as the Cold War. It was "cold" because there was no direct fighting between the two nations; just a lot of threats and spies and secret plans.

Both the U.S.S.R. and the U.S.A. felt that Korea should be united as one country, but they couldn't agree if it should be a democratic government or a communist one. Even though everyone got together to talk about peace and finding a solution, things worked out kind of differently. On June 25, 1950, tons of North Korean troops marched across the 38th Parallel towards Seoul, the capital city of South Korea. They decided that enough time had been spent in talking and that it was time for action. Although there had been lots of little fights before, this one was gigantic, and lots of soldiers were involved.

Two days later, on the 27th of June, the President of South Korea (Syngman Rhee) fled the capital city and established a new headquarters in the southern city of Busan. The next day, the 28th of June, saw a lot of Korean blood spilled onto the streets. The North Korean army arrived in Seoul, and among the many violent acts they carried out was a massacre of 900 doctors, nurses, patients, and wounded soldiers at a hospital in Seoul. For his part, President Syngman Rhee ordered that mass executions of suspected Communists and friends of Communists be carried out. Within just a few months, over 100,000 South Koreans, his fellow citizens, had been killed. It is sad to say, but that number includes many young children and innocent civilians. The bodies were buried in large graves, some of which have still not been found today.

On that same day, President Syngman Rhee ordered that a main bridge leading into Seoul be blown up in order to hold back the North Korean troops that were trying to enter. But there was a problem: the bridge was full of South Korean citizens trying to escape the Communist troops and to head further south. The South Korean army didn't warn anyone about the destruction of the bridge, and they blew it up at 2:30 PM on June 28, when there were more than 4,000 refugees walking across it. Over 800 people died in the blast and in the bridge collapse, and part of the South Korean army was trapped on the other side.

June 28 was a day when a lot of Korean blood was spilled on the ground, entirely by other Koreans. The question was: how much longer would the killing go on?

As you may know, after World War Two was finished, a special organization was set up: The United Nations. This organization was to be a place where governments could get together to talk about their problems without having to go to war. What did the United Nations think about the North Korean army's invasion of the South? They condemned it and sent troops (made up mostly of Americans, along with some British, Canadian, and Australian soldiers) to stop the fighting and to unite the peninsula. On June 27, 1950, the Security Council of the United Nations passed resolution 83, which included the following statement:

> "[The Security Council] recommends that the Members of the United Nations furnish such assistance to the Republic of Korea as may be necessary to repel the armed attack and to restore international peace and security in the area.[3]"

Meanwhile, the U.S.S.R. decided that it would secretly help the Communist North to win, while the Allies (mainly made up of Americans) decided that they would go and fight for the Democratic South.

The international community had officially become a part of the Korean War.

---

[3] Image source: http://www.unhcr.org/refworld/docid/3b00f20a2c.html

Chapter 2: Why Did the Korean War Happen?

Have you ever played with a set of dominos? Well, what happens if you line them all up and then push over the one at the end? You would probably see something like the following happen:

One single domino that falls can trigger a chain reaction and make all the dominos fall.[4]

---

[4] Image source: http://insureblog.blogspot.com/2012/07/dominos-

A lot of people around the world thought that Korea was like a domino. How so? Well, do you remember the tensions that existed between the U.S.S.R. and the United States? The United States didn't want Communism to spread to any more countries, and the U.S.S.R. thought that lots of countries should try this new type of government. In fact, the civil war in China that had been fought just after World War Two ended up bringing in a Communist government. The United States, along with some other countries, was worried that if Korea became a Communist country than other nearby Asian lands would also, and maybe all of Europe would, as well.

The world had seen that while Communism had the goal of helping people, the citizens were the ones who often ended up suffering. For example, in 1932 the Soviet Union experienced a terrible famine, during which some six million Soviets died as a result of not having enough food. The government had not been able to manage the Communist system well, and the farmers themselves had to give away all the food that they grew to people living in the big cities. The farmers were often left with nothing for themselves. The United States was worried that if Communism were to spread, then many more people would be forced to suffer like those Soviets had during the famine.

The goal of the United States, as stated exceptionally clearly by President Truman, became one of

part-deux.html

—

"containment", or in other words, of keeping the Soviets from gaining any new ground in the future or from spreading their politics to other countries. When the Korean War broke out, Truman was afraid that the Soviets were going to try to get Korea united under a Communist government and that they would then move on to Japan, which had become a new stronghold and base for Democracy in Asia.

It was also feared that the war in Korea would get larger and larger, eventually becoming a global conflict (like what had happened in World War One). It was hoped that by the United Nations getting involved early in the fighting then other nations (like China and the U.S.S.R.) wouldn't get involved and make the whole thing get bigger than it had to be.

Truman initially referred to the U.N. intervention in the Korean civil war as a "police action". It was hoped that the fighting would be minimal, and it would be more like a teacher trying to break up a fight between two boys on the playground. Also, Truman thought that this war, if it was allowed to escalate and involve a lot of other nations, would become a threat to the young organization of the United Nations. After all, if no one took what the U.N. said seriously when talking about a small war in Asia, how would it ever be able to prevent a Third World War?

As you can see, what started as a fight between the two halves of one country quickly became something much larger. The Americans thought that the Soviets were trying to expand their politics into neighboring countries, and the Soviets thought that the Americans were too blinded by their own prejudices and greed to see that there were many ways of doing things. The Soviets also thought that the Americans wanted to conquer the whole world. Although neither side was ready for a direct war, it soon became clear that they would use Korea as a sort of "proxy war". Do you know what a proxy war is?

A proxy is like a representative. Sometimes, when an executive has to vote in an important company meeting, but he can't make it, he will send a "proxy" to vote for him. So a proxy war is when two countries use representatives (other armies) to fight their war for them. The Soviets used the North Koreans, and the Americans used the South Koreans. Both sides gave money, supplies, and advice to the armies, and the Americans even sent thousands of soldiers to Korea to fight.

This proxy war never escalated to become a Third World War, but that doesn't mean that it was an unimportant war. It was important to the world and to the Korean people. In fact, what do you think the Korean people thought about the Soviets and the Americans using them like chess pieces?

Do you remember how there was a lot of fighting just before the war broke out? Thousands of Koreans died because they couldn't get along. Some wanted a Communist government and others wanted a democratic government. Normally, the best way to decide something is for everyone to get together and talk about it or vote on it in a free election. However, the foreign power that was occupying the northern part of the Korean Peninsula (the U.S.S.R.) didn't allow free elections in 1948. The people had been ruled for thirty years by the Japanese, were never listened to, and now it felt like history was repeating itself.

In fact, when the decision was made for the Soviets, and the Americans to occupy the two halves of Korea guess how many Koreans they asked about it? None! That's right. Even in that pivotal moment when the future of Korea would be decided, the Korean people still were not able to have a voice in the decision!

As a result, even though the south was officially "Democratic", that didn't mean that everyone was 100% on board with the decisions made by the president. And in the North, some people didn't want the Soviets pushing them around; but they actually didn't have a choice in the matter.

When the fighting finally started in June of 1950, the soldiers on each side were scared, but some were more prepared than others for the long months and years of fighting that awaited them.

Chapter 3: What Happened During the Korean War?

An American soldier sits on a captured hill during a quiet moment of the Korean War in 1951.[5]

As we have seen already, the Korean War started with a day of horrific violence. Men, women, and children were gunned down by their fellow citizens, and it seemed like there was no escape. Wherever the citizens turned, especially near the capital, it seemed like there were explosions, gunshots, and screams of

[5] Image source: http://en.wikipedia.org/wiki/File:Korean_War_HA-SN-98-07010.jpg

pain and sadness. When the United Nations authorized the Americans and others to intervene, it was hoped that the arrival of more forces would calm things down in the region and help to stabilize the peninsula. Unfortunately, when the help finally arrived, it was too little, too late.

The first American troops were quickly moved over from nearby Japan, and they soon arrived in Korea on July 1. The first battle of the Korean War that included American soldiers was on July 5, 1950, near the city of Osan, south of the capital city of Seoul. There were a little more than 500 American soldiers, and their job was mainly to hold the line to keep the North Korean troops from moving further south. The Americans didn't want to lose complete control of the southern part of the peninsula and were hoping to land more troops there soon. The soldiers that fought in the Battle of Osan were from the 1st Battalion, 21st Infantry of the United States Army.

The men of the 1st Battalion, 21st Infantry were not fully prepared for the war (in terms of equipment and experience) and they were too few to be fighting against such a large amount of enemy combatants. In fact, five out of every six soldiers had never fired a weapon in war. When the giant North Korean army came out to meet them with 36 tanks and 5,000 infantry, the American soldiers were only able to hold out for about three hours before receiving the order to evacuate as we saw in the introduction. Some of the soldiers didn't get the order in time, and they had to leave behind their heavy weapons (which were later used against them) and their wound comrades in order to escape.

The Battle of Osan made the Americans realize that they were dealing with a large, well-equipped and well-organized enemy. This was not going to be an easy walk in the park; this was going to be a difficult war.

The soldiers arrived in July, during what was to be a terribly hot summer. There was not enough water, so the men had to drink the irrigation water from nearby rice fields, water that had been contaminated with human waste. Many of the soldiers got sick, and it was hard for them to fight well. As for the South Korean soldiers themselves, many of them were also scared and inexperienced on the battlefield. For a time, it seemed like the North Koreans were going to win practically without a fight. In fact, one of the men high up in the North Korean government predicted that they would have a complete victory by November.

By August, the American soldiers (and their allies from the United Nations) had been pushed all the way down to Nakdong River, near the city of Pusan. The North Korean troops now were in control of about 90% of the peninsula and were closing in fast. The Americans decided that it was time to push back.

The first step was to stop the North Korean war machine that was marching unstoppably forward. The United States Air Force used jet-fighters to bomb enemy positions, to destroy railroads and bridges, and to keep the troops from advancing. Then, tanks and soldiers were sent directly to Korea from the United States, and by early September, the Americans and their allies outnumbered the North Korean army about 180,000 to 100,000. Things were finally starting to look like they would start going in favor of the South Korean government and the U.N. soldiers.

On September 15, a large-scale offensive was launched to the north, almost 100 miles behind the North Korean battle lines. With support from naval ships and the air force, General Douglas MacArthur (the American General in charge of the Korean War) landed some 40,000 troops onto the beach of Inchon. During four days, these soldiers killed about 1,350 North Korean troops and started a massive retreat.

Some 40,000 soldiers and tanks participated in the Battle of Inchon.[6]

With the rest of the army pushing up from the south, the North Korean soldiers were soon retreating in a thoroughly disorganized way, leaving many men behind and even leaving their capital city, Pyongyang, vulnerable. On September 25, Seoul was recaptured by the Americans and South Korean forces.

The fight kept moving further and further north, and on October 7, the Americans and their allies crossed the 38th Parallel, officially in enemy territory. China had previously threatened that it would be upset and would try to stop the Americans if that happened, but their warnings weren't actually listened to. As we will see, China was about to get involved and change the way the war was fought.

The American soldiers kept pushing further and further north, and it looked as if the war might end soon, with a victory for the Democratic South. However, as American troops neared the Chinese border, they were surprised to learn that some two hundred thousand Chinese troops had crossed the border and were fighting for the North Koreans. On October 25, 1950, the Chinese troops had entered Korea. They, like the North Koreans, were supported by a Communist government. The three nations shared the same political ideas, and now they shared the same enemy. Although not everyone in the Chinese government wanted war with the United States, the most powerful people (including

[6] Image source: http://en.wikipedia.org/wiki/Battle_of_Inchon

Premier Zhou Enlai) did, and so China entered the war.

General MacArthur had thought that the Chinese would never enter the war, and that if they did they would be slaughtered by the Air Force. But the Chinese used tactics to avoid being seen by the Americans. They only marched at night, used camouflage during the day, and froze in place whenever a plane flew overhead. As a result, the Chinese entered by surprise and on November 1 they were able to fight against and push back the U.S. soldiers before retreating back into the mountains. In a series of offensives, the Chinese and the North Koreans were able to, time after time, push the Americans and U.N. soldiers all the way down south, past the city of Seoul.

During the month of December, the American and South Korean troops were the ones retreating. During one mass evacuation in December, one boat, built to carry 12 passengers, carried over 14,000 refugees to safety, without losing a single one of them to the bullets being shot by North Korea soldiers. The *SS Meredith Victory* holds the record for the largest single evacuation by one ship, and many thousands of innocent people's lives were saved by the bravery of the men sailing that ship.

During an especially strong offensive, the city of Seoul was officially recaptured by the North Koreans on January 4. At this moment, General MacArthur started seriously thinking about using nuclear weapons against the North Korean and Chinese troops. He thought that it might bring a quick end to the war, just as the atom bombs had in Japan during World War Two. The President of the United States didn't agree, but MacArthur thought that since he was the General on the field of battle it was his decision.

During the next few months, the Americans and their allies got better organized, and the North Koreans and Chinese started to have problems getting enough food for their troops. In March of 1951, the Americans and United Nations troops pushed strongly northwards and were able to take back, once again the city of Seoul. In case you are counting, you will see that this makes four times in one year that the city was conquered. The people living there were seriously suffering, and there were only about 200,000 citizens still there (down from around 1.5 million before the war).

When the fighting began to increase again, the Chinese started to make plans to get their Air Force in the action (something that they soon did). The fighting then began to be in the ground and in the air. On April 11, 1951, General MacArthur, who had fought on several occasions with President Truman, was fired from his position and sent to be tried in Washington D.C. He was found guilty of having disobeyed the orders of the President and of bringing China into the war by rushing past the 38th Parallel, even though China had warned the Americans not to do so.

MacArthur had felt that complete victory was the only option, even if it meant a long and costly land war in Asia, even if the war was to be against China. Truman, on the other hand, felt that it would be better to finish the "police action" that they had started: stop the fighting and start an orderly withdrawal of troops. The new General, General Matthew Ridgeway wanted to cooperate with the United Nations, and like President Truman, he wanted to limit the fighting and death and to get the troops home.

By the end of May, the troops had pushed as far north as the 38th Parallel. There, neither side could seem to get the other to budge. After all the fighting, the death, the advances and the retreats, both armies were back where they had started before the war.

Chapter 4: What Was It Like to Be a Kid During the Korean War?

The Korean War saw a lot of terrible things happen to a lot of people. There were innocent people that were killed in the streets or out in the fields, and some were either left in the hot sun or buried in giant pits with thousands of other people. Some of the people killed were even as young as twelve or thirteen years old. What do you think it was like to be a kid back then?

Being a kid in the United States would not have been too much different than now. The strange thing is that not a lot of people talked about the war or wanted to know much about what was going on over in Korea. You see, the American people had just experienced the long, drawn out horror of World War Two. They had been scared of being attacked by Japanese or German submarines, and had even started to get suspicious of Japanese and German people who were American citizens. After the war had ended, everyone kind of wanted to forget about it and move on, just get on with their lives.

When the United Nations Security Council decided to send troops to Korea, several thousand young men went. But the Korean War never had the support of the whole country like World War Two did. It all seemed so far away and hard to understand. It wasn't as easy to grasp like the other war had been, where everyone wanted revenge for Pearl Harbor or to stop Adolf Hitler. This war just seemed unimportant.

As a result, a lot of kids in the United States never quite understood what the war was all about, and there were no grandiose parades or celebrations when it was all over.

Being a kid in Korea would have been totally different.

An American soldier says hello to a Korean child during the war.[7]

As a kid living in Korea during the war, you would have your entire world get ripped apart at the seams. You would have seen neighbors with certain political ideas marched off to be executed, and you would have seen your hometown get destroyed by bombs

[7] Image source: http://www.chrysopeia.com/photo.html

and guns. All kinds of strange people would be marching down the roads, and it would be hard to know who the good guys were and who the bad guys were.

There wouldn't be enough food for everyone, and you would probably see your parents go hungry just so that they could give food to you and your brothers and sisters. Can you imagine seeing the sadness in their eyes as they wondered what the next day would be like?

Being a kid during the Korean War meant a lot of confusion and a lot of questions without answers, no matter where you lived.

Chapter 5: How Did the Korean War End?

By summer of 1951, the soldiers were back at the 38th Parallel, fighting each other with everything they had. Because neither army could make the other one move, they dug trenches and began to fight like the soldiers had fought back in World War One- shooting lots of bullets and bombs at each other, trying to weaken the other side.

Around that time, both sides started to get together to make some sort of a peace agreement, or at least a cease-fire. The main issue that was so hard for them to agree on was what to do with the prisoners of war. Some felt that the prisoners of war should stay where they were at while others felt that the prisoners should be forced to go back to where they came from. It was difficult, because some families had been separated, and they might never get to see each other again.

Another question was what to do with the dead soldiers. Should they be buried where they died, should they be taken home, or should everyone just forget about them? It took some time and lots of meetings, but an armistice (a long term cease-fire while a treaty can be signed) was arranged for and agreed to on July 27, 1953. Some three years after the fighting had started, it was finally about to stop.

An armistice that ended the fighting was signed on July 27, 1953.[8]

The armistice was to ensure that there would be no more fighting, but also that the prisoners of war and dead soldiers could be taken care of. During Operation Big Switch, which began in August, all prisoners of war were exchanged, and they finally got to go back home. Then, during Operation Glory, which began in July of 1954, the remains of fallen soldiers were exchanged and buried with the dignity that they deserved.

The division of Korea was made permanent, and two independent nations, one Communist and one Democratic, were formed. In between them, there was designated a special area called a DMZ, or demilitarized zone (about 2.5 miles wide), that was to act as a sort of buffer between the two nations and to help make sure they didn't start fighting again.

[8] Image source: http://www.nationaljournal.com/pictures-video/nearly-60-years-after-armistice-korean-war-hasn-t-ended-pictures-20120727

North Korean soldiers look south from the DMZ.[9]

So far, although the armistice was meant to be a
temporary halt to the fighting until a treaty could be
signed, it has lasted almost sixty years, and no
substantial fighting has broken out.

[9]   Image   source:
http://en.wikipedia.org/wiki/File:JointSecurityAreaNorthKoreans.jp
g

Chapter 6: What Happened After the Korean War?

The armistice that ended the fighting of the Korean War was signed on July 27, 1953. Some 40,000 American soldiers died, and another 100,000 were wounded. South Korea lost 46,000 soldiers and about 100,000 were wounded. But their losses were small compared with the enemy's. North Korea lost 215,000 troops and another 303,000 were wounded while China lost 400,000 soldiers on the battlefield, and another 486,000 were wounded. When you factor in the civilians who died and those who had to flee their homes because of the war, we can see that there was a lot of tragedy and death during the Korean War.

What has happened in Korea since the fighting stopped?

Although no substantial fighting has broken out since then, both the North and the South have been guilty of starting smaller skirmishes. One that got a lot of worldwide attention happened in 2010, when a North Korean torpedo destroyed a South Korean ship, killing 46 sailors. Because the Northern country has established the reputation of being somewhat reckless and aggressive, the whole world seems to hold its breath whenever events like that happen, wondering if another war is about to break out.

North Korea seems terribly interested in developing powerful rocket engines, which some worry may be the next step towards missiles that can be aimed at targets on the other side of the world. North Korea continues to ignore instructions and threats from the United Nations and continues to stay close to fellow Communist government, China. Time will tell if anything substantial happens in that region in the future.

South Korea, on the other hand, has recovered exceptionally well and is one of the world's largest economies and has a supremely high standard of living.

Surprisingly, some Americans defected (went to the enemy) during the Korean War. 21 American soldiers who had been captured as prisoners of war decided to stay with their captors and start new lives, mainly in China. Although their reasons were all different, some of them decided to stay for love after having met and married a local girl. Others changed their politics and actively supported Communism, never returning to the United States.

When the American soldiers came back home after having fought in the Korean War, some of them were surprised to find that there were no parades, no welcome parties, no visits to the White House to thank them for their service. They had fought for years, and it was like no one even knew what they had been doing or why they had been fighting. As we saw in the first picture, there were men crying because their best friends had died, but they came home to a country that didn't know anything about the sacrifices of them or their fellow soldiers. Can you imagine how they felt? Would you have felt appreciated?

Today, the Korean War is often called the "Forgotten War". Why? Most people don't know much about it, why it happened or who was involved. They don't understand the domino theory or how close the world got to seeing more nuclear bombs used during wartime. Worst of all, they don't realize how many Americans died fighting for the rights of others.

Conclusion

Have you learned something about the Korean War from this handbook? Could you explain it to someone else if they asked you about the war? Let's review some of the main points that we learned.

First, we learned more about what actually caused the Korean War. Did you see how the war actually started as a sort of civil war between the Korean people, but that later other nations got involved? The country had been divided into two parts after World War Two, each one occupied by a foreign power. The north was occupied by the Soviets, and the south by the Americans. When the civil war broke out, it was as if the U.S.A. and the U.S.S.R. were fighting each other through proxies, or representatives. This was one of the first battles of the Cold War.

The next section talked about why the United States and other nations got involved in the civil war of Korea, a nation on the other side of the world. Once North Korea invaded the south, the United Nations got involved and sent troops to stop the fighting, like police officers trying to calm down a rowdy crowd. The United States in particular was worried about something called the "domino theory". Do you remember what the domino theory was? It was a way of thinking that some politicians and citizens in the United States and Europe had. They thought that if one country (like North Korea) could be conquered by the Communists, there other countries would fall one by one, like a series of dominos stacked up in a line. To prevent that, the Americans and their allies felt that North Korea needed to be contained and prevented from taking over South Korea. We also saw how both the U.S.S.R. and China supported the North Koreans, either by sending troops, weapons, money, or advisors.

After that, we learned more about the Korean War itself. Like we saw in the picture at the beginning of this handbook, there were some truly sad moments during the war, like when soldiers lost their friends on the battlefields. The Korean War also saw a lot of civilians get killed in huge massacres. Do you remember who was responsible for many of the deaths? That's right: many of the deaths were Koreans killing Koreans, sometimes people from their own country (like when the bridge was blown up, and many innocent refugees were killed). We saw how the fighting was fierce, but how by the end of the war, everyone was back to where they started from.

The following section showed us what it was like to be a kid living during the Korean War. We used our imaginations to see what it was like to be a kid in the U.S. during the war, and what kinds of things they would have seen and heard about. Do you remember what we saw? We saw that a lot of kids probably wouldn't have understood much about the war because no one actually talked about it. The troops weren't treated like heroes like the veterans of World War Two. We also saw what it would have been like to be a kid living in Korea during the war. As you can probably imagine, it would have been a lot scarier in Korea because of all the fighting and the violence towards innocent civilians.

Next, we saw how the Korean War finally ended. Although the fighting was pretty fierce and tough in the beginning, and although the armies moved around a lot, by the end of the war, things had settled down and everyone wanted the fighting to end. Even so, we saw that it took almost two years for the governments on each side to finally sign the documents to end the fighting. Do you remember what the conditions were that kept the armistice from being signed for so long? The most difficult question was what to do with the prisoners of war. It was finally decided to send everyone back home, and most ended up doing just that.

The final section showed us what the two Koreas (North and South) look like today. We saw that North Korea is still Communist and that they still believe in uniting the two countries under one government. Although the people are poor and don't always have enough to eat, the people are intensely loyal to their leader and to their government. In the South, the economy is doing very well, and life is not much different from the United States. Just about everyone has their own house and a high standard of living. The countries still have skirmishes, and some wonder if there will be another war in the future. We will have to wait and see what happens.

Have you enjoyed learning about Korea from this handbook? It was been an interesting lesson, although it had its sad parts. But why should you care so much about the Korean War? Although some people think that this war was not too prominent, what do you think: should we look at it like that? Not at all. We should always remember how much the soldiers sacrificed to help the Korean people, and how important it was to stop the North Koreans. While not everything about the "domino theory" was 100% accurate, it is always important that people be allowed to choose for themselves what kind of government they want to live under. No one should ever be forced to obey laws and rules that they don't agree with. It was wrong for the North Koreans to try to force their fellow Koreans to think like they did, and the American soldiers fought to stop it from happening.

Although it ended almost sixty years ago, the legend of the Korean War should never be forgotten. Helping out someone else, being willing to die for them, is the most beautiful thing that one human can do for another.

The first state-sponsored memorial (in Washington state) to those who died in the Korean War.[10]

---

[10]   Image   source:
http://www.ga.wa.gov/visitor/korean/koreanwar.htm

Made in the USA
Las Vegas, NV
03 August 2021